For Bill and Allison, and for John, who
reminds me an awful lot of George (except for the
forgetting stuff part, of course)
—K. W.

For Louise
—R. B.

First published in the United States of America in July 2017
by Bloomsbury Children's Books
www.bloomsbury.com

Bloomsbury is a registered trademark of Bloomsbury Publishing Plc

For information about permission to reproduce selections from this book, write to
Permissions, Bloomsbury Children's Books, 1385 Broadway, New York, New York 10018
Bloomsbury books may be purchased for business or promotional use. For information on bulk purchases please contact
Macmillan Corporate and Premium Sales Department at specialmarkets@macmillan.com

Library of Congress Cataloging-in-Publication Data
Names: Wolff, Kathy, author. | Byrne, Richard, illustrator.
Title: What George forgot / by Kathy Wolff ; illustrated by Richard Byrne.
Description: New York : Bloomsbury, 2017.
Summary: George is great at remembering things. When it's time to get ready for school, he remembers to wake up his
family and put on his favorite fuzzy sweater and brand-new superhero watch. So why does George feel like he is forgetting
something? Readers know what George forgot, but will he ever figure it out?
Identifiers: LCCN 2016036832 (print) • LCCN 2016049489 (e-book)
ISBN 978-1-61963-871-6 (hardcover) • ISBN 978-1-61963-872-3 (e-book) • ISBN 978-1-61963-873-0 (e-PDF)
Subjects: | CYAC: Memory—Fiction. | Humorous stories. | BISAC: JUVENILE FICTION / Humorous Stories. | JUVENILE
FICTION / Family / General (see also headings under Social Issues). | JUVENILE FICTION / School & Education.
Classification: LCC PZ7.1.W628 Wh 2017 (print) | LCC PZ7.1.W628 (e-book) | DDC [E]—dc23
LC record available at https://lccn.loc.gov/2016036832

Art created with Richard's favorite pencil, the Faber-Castell Pitt Graphite Pure 2900 9B,
and then colored digitally in Adobe Illustrator
Typeset in Minya Nouvelle
Book design by Richard Byrne and Jessie Gang
Printed in China by Leo Paper Products, Heshan, Guangdong
2 4 6 8 10 9 7 5 3 1

All papers used by Bloomsbury Publishing, Inc., are natural, recyclable products
made from wood grown in well-managed forests. The manufacturing processes
conform to the environmental regulations of the country of origin.

What George Forgot

Kathy Wolff   ILLUSTRATED BY Richard Byrne

BLOOMSBURY
NEW YORK   LONDON   OXFORD   NEW DELHI   SYDNEY

George always remembered
never to forget *anything.*

Except when he forgot.

And today he just had this
funny feeling that there was
something he was forgetting.

Had he remembered to wake up?

Yes.

And make his bed, first thing?

Yes.

Had he remembered to wake:

His mom with a running bear hug? →

His dad with a hairy-foot tickle? ←

And his sister with her morning wake-up call?

Yes, yes, and yes.

He'd gotten dressed in his favorite fuzzy sweater.

And put on his brand-new superhero watch.

He'd even remembered clean undies.

What could George be forgetting?

Here is something George *definitely* didn't forget:

Breakfast.

Also, his
pre-breakfast
banana . . .

and his post-
breakfast nuts.

(George ALWAYS remembered to eat.)

He'd remembered to tell his dad his three funniest pirate jokes.

Gotcha, matey! Arrr.

And even took his two chewy vitamins.

Check

and

check.

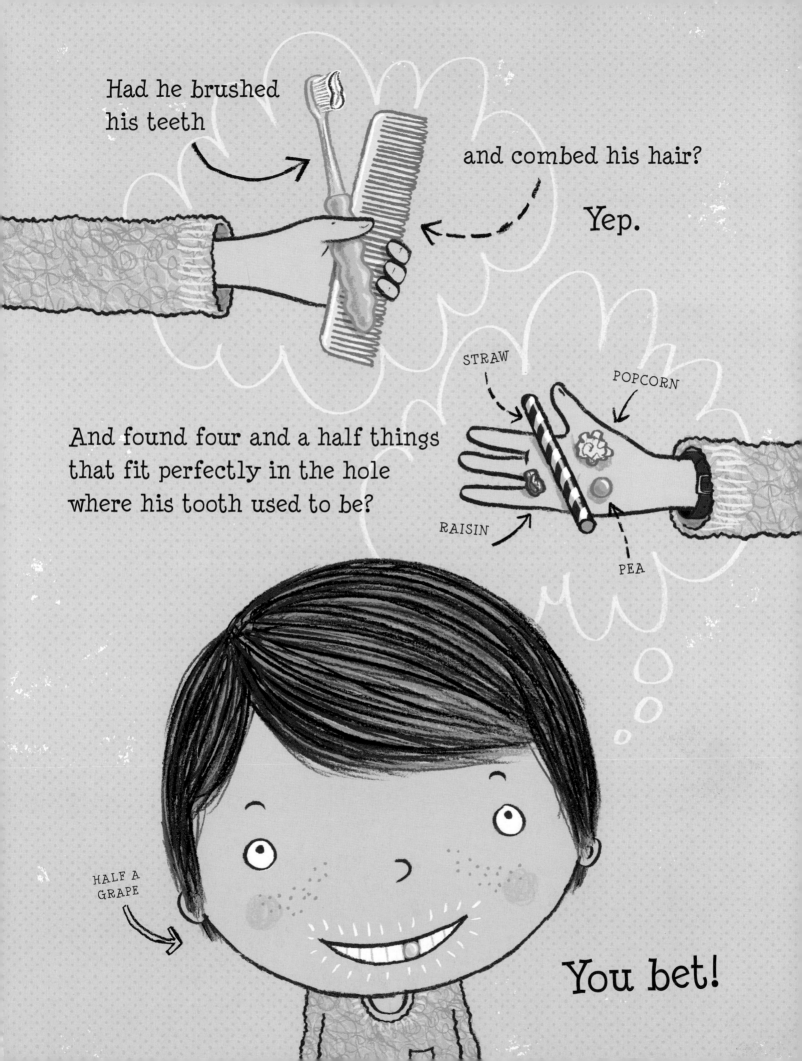

Had he brushed his teeth

and combed his hair?

Yep.

STRAW

POPCORN

And found four and a half things that fit perfectly in the hole where his tooth used to be?

RAISIN

PEA

HALF A GRAPE

You bet!

He knew he'd definitely remembered not to forget to:

gargle,

spit,

shave.

No, just kidding. George is just a kid—he doesn't need to remember to shave! (He only does that on Tuesdays.)

So **what** was George forgetting?

Had he remembered to:

Use the
bathroom?

Yes.

Flush? Yes.

Wash his hands? Yes.

(With soap?)

Oh, right. Yes.

Turn **off** the faucet?

Yes. (Just in time!)

Had he beaten his Slinky down the stairs?

Twice!

He'd fed Earl,

brushed Earl,

and given him a
nice, long belly rub.

(Earl would *never*
let him forget that.)

Had he remembered to remind his mom to pack a dessert in his lunch?

Definitely.

And rock-paper-scissored his sister for the blinky yo-yo for show-and-tell?

Two out of three!

And invented a flying backpack-putting-on machine?!?!

Why, yes he had.

WAHOO!!!

George's flying backpack-putting-on machine

So what could George
possibly be forgetting?

He just had this feeling there
was **something** . . .

OH!!!

Silly George.

How could he have almost
forgotten . . .

Good thing he remembered not to forget *those* before he left the house.